Div

Divergent Series, Book 1

Veronica Roth

SUMMARY & ANALYTICAL REVIEW

BY

Book*Sense

Note to Readers:

This is an unofficial Summary & Analysis of Divergent by Veronica Roth. You are encouraged to buy the full version.

TABLE OF CONTENTS

INTRODUCTION

Bestselling author Veronica Roth emerges in glory in Divergent, the first novel in a near-future dystopia that promises its readers more enthralling action to come. In the book, Roth relates the story of Beatrice "Tris" Prior in a gripping story of passage into adulthood in a society evocative of the fears voiced by Aldous Huxley, George Orwell, environmental activists and those who regard with trepidation the increasing miniaturization and prevalence of technology. It is a compelling read not only for the young adults of its intended audience, but also for their parents, those who teach them and those who have themselves faced the frightening passage from the safety and security of a childhood home into the nuanced, shaded and too often shady broader societies of adulthood.

Below appears a review of Veronica Roth's Divergent, discussion of its milieu, a list of significant characters, a summary of the book and an analysis of Beatrice "Tris" before a few concluding comments.

BOOK REVIEW

Veronica Roth's 2011 novel Divergent is a science-fiction young adult novel set in a near-future Chicago that has experienced both environmental and social upheaval. It follows the emergence of Beatrice "Tris" Prior into adulthood as she leaves the faction—a group somewhere between political party, religious orientation, civic society, caste and college—of her birth for that of her choice. She is pulled not only into the typical struggles of late adolescence and early adulthood, but also into political struggles that quickly become armed and violent. While she is able to put a halt to the most overt actions, she does so at the cost of both her native and adopted factions and the splintering of the society in which they exist, leaving her and those in her company effectively exiled and adrift in an unfriendly world.

Like many young-adult works, Divergent is in many respects a typical coming-of-age novel. The typical tropes of the genre are in place. The protagonist leaves home to join another group of people who will train her how to live as one of them (mimetic of going to college as many of the book's primary readers will do in short order). In the process of learning how to fit in among them, she finds that she is special in a way much of the broader society regards as dangerous but that ultimately allows her to resist the constraints of society and escape from its restrictions. The book thus rearticulates the perpetual struggle of the emergent young adult, who strives for self-identification and desires uniqueness while struggling against the perceived constraints of an unfair and fundamentally flawed society. The adherence to generic conventions does serve to make the text accessible to readers conditioned to expect such devices from the fiction assigned to young adult readership, which may help the reception of the social commentaries made in the text.

One such is the assertion that the protection of a society comes at the cost of being constrained by it. Roth makes the point several times in the novel that in a society which operates well, the protections and privileges of membership in the prestige-carrying groups necessarily comes at the cost of obedience to those groups. Setting aside the constraints they impose carries a concomitant loss of the benefits accorded to those who accept the constraints. In short, people cannot have full autonomy and access to the benefits of obedience—a message that bears repeating. Another such message is that wishing to join a group is not the same as having the acceptance of that group. Bodies of people make their own decisions as to whom they accept, and they impose (sometimes ludicrous) conditions for achieving that acceptance. Yet another, and perhaps the most important in the novel, is the idea that self-sacrifice enables greatness. It is from a willingness to sacrifice life and happiness for the betterment of others that the purportedly dangerous divergence of the novel's title most often grows, and it is that divergence that allows for such salvation as Roth describes. The communitarian drive is thus emphasized, which emphasis is one that the youth to whom the book is addressed and the rest of those who read it do well to see again and again.

THE SETTING FOR THE STORY

Divergent is set in Chicago in the near future. The grand buildings of downtown, such as the former Sears Tower, are intact enough to be used, as are the famous elevated trains, although much is in disrepair. The streets are in ruins, power is tightly rationed and there are pronounced holes in many of the civic edifices. Technology, particularly in cognitive sciences, drug therapies and genetic food modification, is advanced beyond that available when the novel debuted. Society has fractured, with the city being isolated from the rest of the country and divided into six groups: the five emblematically named ruling factions —Abnegation, Amity, and Candor, Dauntless and Erudite— and the factionless underclass. Each of the factions prizes a particular virtue: Abnegation, selflessness; Amity, friendship; Candor, honesty; Dauntless, courage, and Erudite, learning. The selflessness ascribed to Abnegation means that overall governance is by a council of some fifty Abnegation members, although not all are pleased by the arrangement. Children are raised by their native factions until age sixteen, at which point they are tested and choose a faction to join; not all are accepted, giving rise to the underclass, which performs the menial functions of the remaining Chicago society and live on the charity of the factions.

MAIN & SECONDARY CHARACTER LIST

Beatrice "Tris" Prior is the clear protagonist; she narrates the action of Divergent and is the focus of it. She is joined by many others in the text:

- Al

Native Candor and fellow Dauntless initiate with Tris, rejected romantic interest

- Andrew Prior

Abnegation social leader and father of Tris

- Caleb Prior

Erudite initiate and brother of Tris

- Christina

Native Candor and fellow Dauntless initiate with Tris, early Dauntless friend

- Drew

Native Erudite and fellow Dauntless initiate with Tris,

early Dauntless foe and accomplice of Peter

• Edward

Native Erudite and fellow Dauntless initiate with Tris, early Dauntless wunderkind, romantically entangled with Myra

• Eric

Native Erudite, Dauntless leader, Divergent hunter

• Jeanine Matthews

Erudite leader and antagonist lynchpin

• Marcus

Abnegation social leader, father of Tobias and child abuser

• Molly "the Tank" Atwood

Native Candor and fellow Dauntless initiate with Tris, early Dauntless foe and accomplice of Peter

• Myra

Native Erudite and fellow Dauntless initiate with Tris, romantically entangled with Edward

• Natalie Prior

Native Dauntless and mother of Tris

• Peter

Native Candor and fellow Dauntless initiate with Tris, early Dauntless foe

• Tobias "Four,"

Dauntless initiate trainer, former Abnegation and love interest for Tris

• Tori

Native Erudite, Dauntless tattoo artist, early examiner of Tris and first warning of the dangers of Divergence

• Uriah

Native Dauntless initiate, friend of Tris

• Will

Native Erudite and fellow Dauntless initiate with Tris, early Dauntless friend

BOOK OVERVIEW & STORY ANALYSIS

Below appears a summary of the text, with some analytical comments interspersed.

Chapter 1

The novel opens with Beatrice getting a haircut not long after her sixteenth birthday. The note is made that her native faction does not celebrate birthdays, avoiding them as indulgences. Mention is made of the forthcoming Choosing Ceremony that determines future life courses and that Beatrice is leaving her native Abnegation. Soon after, Beatrice and her brother, Caleb, are riding the bus to school. Other factions begin to be introduced: the stark and honest Candor, the train-riding "hellion" Dauntless. Setting explication is made, and all factions are named. Arrogance of the Erudite and the dismissive attitudes towards Abnegation are evidenced, as is the brazenness of the Dauntless.

Chapter 2

The aptitude tests which inform the Choosing Ceremony take place. Abnegation volunteers staff most of them, although other factions test Abnegation natives. The secretive nature of the tests is noted. The pervasive control of faction life is also noted. Beatrice admits to nervousness about the exercise amid discussing her non-fit among the Abnegation. She also sits for her test, which is administered via electrodes and drugs; it consists of a series of hallucinations meant to judge root impulses.

Chapter 3

Beatrice emerges from the test to find the test administrator, the Dauntless Tori, confused by the demonstrated results. The plight of the factionless is noted. The inconclusiveness of Beatrice's results is discussed, as is the dangerous divergence they reveal. Beatrice returns home afoot, encountering ruined parts of Chicago and the factionless along the way; their menial subservience is noted. An encounter with a factionless man allows reassertion of Beatrice's too-young appearance and the importance of the Choosing Ceremony.

Chapter 4

Beatrice reaches her native home, describing the sector of the city in which it stands. She waits for her brother, who soon arrives and is suspicious both of Beatrice's early arrival and her story covering it. He is somewhat distracted by flirtation, and he and Beatrice soon retreat into the house. There, they prepare the evening meal, and after they are joined by their parents, they discuss the events of the day. The political leadership of the factions is noted, as is the irregularity and shame attached to children who leave their native factions at the Choosing Ceremony. Tobias is mentioned, and Beatrice goes to bed considering her choice.

Chapter 5

The next day, Beatrice and others go to the Choosing Ceremony; she remarks upon her continued nervousness. The setup of the Ceremony is described, as are the elemental significances associated with the factions: stone for Abnegation, soil for Amity, air for Candor, fire for Dauntless and water for Erudite. Choosing involves bloodletting onto the appropriate element. The falsity of choice among predetermined options receives passing comment. More explication is given to the underpinnings of the social paradigm informing the milieu; the factions each exist to redress a single failing of human personality. The prime importance of the factions is reasserted, and Beatrice is surprised by her brother's choice of Erudite. She considers remaining in Abnegation, but ultimately chooses Dauntless.

Chapter 6

Beatrice follows other Dauntless initiates out of the Choosing Ceremony. She comments on her emotional upheaval at the choice and her confusion at the actions of the Dauntless leaving the ceremony. One of her fellow initiates fails to even attempt the first train-jump and is thus expelled into factionlessness. Beatrice meets Christina and considers her brother before the second train-jump to Dauntless headquarters. Beatrice succeeds, but not all do. Beatrice then is the first to make the leap into the headquarters proper, surprising her fellow initiates. At that point, she takes a new name: Tris.

Chapter 7

The Dauntless initiates who transfer in from other factions are gathered into a single group and their training at the hands of Four begins. The Dauntless headquarters is described, and Tris wonders about the lack of elderly among them. They are brought to a dining hall, and Tris has her first hamburger. She is introduced to Eric, who intimidates her. After dinner, Eric escorts the initiates to their quarters, describing the training to come—and the consequences of failure. Later, in the night, Tris deals with her emotional upheaval as others in her initiate cadre deal with their own. The emotional instability of Al is suggested.

Chapter 8

Training commences with firearms practice. Four lays out standards and training patterns, shaming Peter in the process of doing so. After, at lunch, there is discussion among the initiates of their former lives. Following that, hand-to-hand combat training begins. Four gives Tris specific instruction meant to compensate for her slighter stature. Once the session ends, several initiates opt to get tattoos. Along the way, Christina takes Tris for a bit of a makeover, and they soon arrive at Tori's tattoo shop. Tris tries to broach the topic of divergence, but is rejected and offered a tattoo to sidetrack the discussion. She opts for three ravens flying toward her heart.

Chapter 9

The narrative resumes with hand-to-hand combat training, the first day of actual fighting. Christina discusses with Tris the evils of Peter, Drew and Molly as Al and Will fight. The open antagonism between Christina and the group is noted. As the fight winds down, Eric calls for more, saying that the fight must continue until one participant no longer can. This draws rebuke from Four, and Will renews his efforts, only to have Al knock him unconscious. Will is taken from the training room, and Christina and Molly fight. Christina does not fare well in the fight, offering her concession. This draws the ire of Eric, who inflicts a sadistic punishment upon her.

Chapter 10

Tris wakes from a dream of Christina's punishment and soon finds her sleeping arrangements vandalized. After a brief antagonistic exchange with Peter, she works to clean up; Al helps her, and the two discuss Will. The next day in hand to hand training, Tris finds herself paired against Peter and receives uncomfortable advice in dealing with him. Her fight against Peter starts badly and does not improve. Tris wakes up in the infirmary, where her friends are either in treatment or in attendance on those who are. Noted is an upcoming training exercise, and Al makes some of his romantic feelings for Tris known. After some consideration, Tris opts to return to her quarters rather than remain in the infirmary.

Chapter 11

Tris wakes only belatedly and with help the next day. Christina chivvies her to the training exercise, which involves a train ride away from the headquarters and the city center. Some indication of Tris's nascent feelings for Four is given. Some discussion of Dauntless duties and positions is offered; noted is that the gates the Dauntless guard open from the outside. Four offers enigmatic advice.

Chapter 12

Tris reaches her bed after another day of training, having been victorious in a fight. Eric enters to roust the initiates for another training exercise—a paintball match of capture the flag. Tris is placed on Four's team, as are most of the more lithe people present. Some setting clues are given, as are some of the philosophical underpinnings of Dauntless. Will begins to take some command of the situation, and Tris opts to scout from high ground. Along the way, more aspects of old Dauntless ideology are discussed. The scouting works, and Four and his team are able to formulate and execute a winning strategy.

Chapter 13, 14 & 15

Training resumes the next morning with knives. Tris and Peter exchange barbs. Al performs poorly and is punished; Tris takes his place. After, Four offers more enigmatic advice to Tris.

Soon after, as Visiting Day approaches, Tris examines her body closely, finding it muscled and hard; Peter, Drew and Molly accost her, and Tris determines to hurt them. At training, she has the opportunity to fight Molly, which goes well for her; Molly is left bloody on the ground.

Tris narrates her experience of Visiting Day. Eric admonishes the initiates about cross-faction fraternization. Tris sees that her mother has come, unexpectedly. Inter-faction tension is remarked upon as being high. Tris's mother meets Four and speaks with him. After, more evidence of tension emerges. Shortly, clues emerge that indicate Tris's mother is native Dauntless and that she is aware of Tris's divergence. Tris's mother also asks Tris to tell Caleb to research the simulation serum.

Chapter 16

Tris returns to her quarters to find Al. He is contemplative and questioning his choice to try for Dauntless. Differences between older and newer Dauntless standards are mentioned. Al's romantic feelings emerge in earnest, and Tris asserts to herself that Al is only a friend. Later, the initiates discuss their first-stage rankings. The scores come out, and Tris finds herself ranked sixth of the nine transferred initiates. Other rankings give cause for worry. After, Tris contemplates her mother's decision to transfer factions until she is disturbed by a shriek: Edward has been stabbed in the eye. Only Drew and Peter are absent from the commotion. As Tris cleans up, she and Christina realize that the attack will not be punished, chilling them. Edward and Myra withdraw from consideration, going into factionless exile together.

Chapter 17 & 18

Tris is outside the dormitory where Edward was stabbed. Uriah sees her and invites her on a native Dauntless ritual. She goes along, pushing herself and entering the Hancock Building to ride a zip line from its roof. After, Tris finds that the Erudite have been asking questions about Abnegation among the Dauntless.

The second stage of initiation begins with some antagonism between the native and transfer initiates. The actual trial is revealed to be simulations of fear experiences meant to teach initiates to regulate their fear responses so that they can think and act appropriately. The simulation comes along with a small transmitter. Tris goes through an attack by birds until she can snap herself out of the simulation. Four reveals the extent of some of his own fears before musing on the meaning of courage.

Chapter 19

Tris emerges into an announced report on Abnegation. She grows angry but is dissuaded from violence by Will, and both are distracted by Christina's decision to get a tattoo. Tris joins her; both are marked with the Dauntless emblem. Al accompanies them, and Tris notices a despondency about him. They encounter a drunk Four and then head to dinner, with Will and the others teasing Tris.

Chapter 20

Tris endures another simulation. There is an irregularity in it, and her Divergence is revealed to Four. After, Tris seeks out Tori, who finally reveals some of the worry about the Divergent; they are uniquely self-aware and self-possessed, such that domination works poorly upon them. Tris is warned to be careful.

Chapter 21

Tris resumes narration several days later, during which time, more reports condemning Abnegation emerge. Tris becomes aware of the physical changes working upon her. Christina has continued to ply Tris's friendship, and the fear testing has continued. Later, in the setup for another simulation test, Tris asks Four after his family. He refuses to answer, and after the test, Tris muses on the effects the testing has on her fellow initiates. Soon after, stage two rankings are published; Tris is ranked first, and she is aware that she is in danger because of it. Reactions from her fellow initiates are mixed. Later, Uriah encounters her and takes her to the other native initiates. Internal tensions are discussed. Four arrives, and he is alone with her in short order, offering her encouragement. Later, Tris returns to the dormitory, and during the night, she overhears discussion of the Divergent before being attacked by Peter, Drew and Al. Four rescues her.

Chapter 22 & 23

Tris awakens in Four's quarters. The two bond somewhat after the event.

Tris remain in Four's quarters overnight; she wonders about him. The next morning, she wakes with bruises and returns to the dining hall, sitting with Will, Uriah and Christina. Al is absent, and the others ask after the previous night's events. Tris tells them, and she realizes that she can easily be killed by those in power. Four calls the transfer initiates, and Christina apologizes for an earlier slight against Tris. Four leads them to the fear landscape, explaining it. Later, upon returning to quarters, Tris and her companions find Al. He seeks to apologize for his actions, which Tris rebuffs harshly.

Chapter 24

Tris is awakened from a dream of her mother by Christina, who reports that Al has been found, an evident suicide. Tris runs from the scene and later finds herself being given peppermint tea by Tori. Factional differences in funereal rites are noted, and Tris finds herself amid the Dauntless memorial rite. It sickens her, and she leaves, only to be encountered by Four. He tries to guide her, warning her as far as he can. More perceived dangers of Divergence are noted. Four reveals some of his psychology and kisses Tris on the forehead.

Chapter 25

Later, after getting another tattoo, Tris is joined by Will and Christina at the edge of a chasm. The three toss copies of Erudite anti-Abnegation reports into it and discuss political tensions. Tris spots Four and follows him; he reveals his self-mortification ritual. Tris admits feelings for Four, and she realizes why he carries the name.

Chapter 26 &27

Tris continues with Four, discussing matters. They find a secluded location where they can speak largely privately. He muses on the link between selflessness and bravery. Soon, the two act upon mutual attraction.

Tris returns to her friends and the training. The initiates face the fear landscape in a training mode, dealing with one trainer's fears. Tris experiences the trainer's fear as her own and slaps Four as he maintains the façade of being a trainer.

Chapter 28

Tris is outside the Dauntless compound and takes one of the trains to visit Caleb among the Erudite. She is able to find him and pass along their mother's message, but she is escorted to the lair of an Erudite leader and interrogated. Tris manages to handle herself well, and it taken back to Dauntless by car—and to censure. Eric is poised to punish her, but Four intervenes and Tris lies herself out of the situation. After a brief conversation, she returns to the dormitory and her friends—who are having their own romantic interludes. One of Christina's fears is revealed. That evening, Tris meets Four, where they have a romantic liaison—and note that Erudite headquarters is lit in defiance of statute. They discuss the increasing political tension and the seemingly forthcoming war against Abnegation.

Chapter 29, 30 & 31

Tris contemplates difference in faction initiation rituals as she approaches her own fear landscape and induction into Dauntless. She is the last of her group to go through it.

Tris faces her fear landscape. She manages to defeat each challenge, albeit with increasing difficulty as the test continues.

Tris emerges from the landscape and is greeted by Dauntless leaders Eric injects her with a purported tracking device. She and Four leave the throng for his quarters. They have a bit of a spat before musing on the various factions' virtues and returning to one another's arms.

Chapter 32 & 33

Four and Tris join the induction banquet. Tris joins her friends, who quiz her about her actions. Rankings are listed, and Tris is first. Molly and Drew are ejected from Dauntless. Suddenly, Tris realizes how the war against Abegnation will begin: the injected transmitters.

Tris awakens in the night to find that the attack has begun. The transmitters have rendered the Dauntless automatons—save for the Divergent among them. Tris moves along with the mass of mind-controlled Dauntless as they begin their assault and meets Tobias. The two move to intercept the assault as best they may, and encounter the Dauntless leaders in a tense standoff that leaves them captured and Tris shot.

Chapter 34

The Dauntless forces march Four and Tris to the leaders and Jeanine Matthews. She interrogates them, then moves to subdue Four and have Tris eliminated. Erudite, through Jeanine, is revealed as wanting to exercise total control. Four attempts to kill Jeanine but is prevented and injected with the new subdual method. Tris is removed.

Chapter 35 & 36

She wakes in the dark in a tank like that of her fears. Tris contemplates her own death but is saved from it by her mother—who is herself Divergent, problematic because uncontrollable and multifaceted. Tris's mother tells her to seek out her father and brother before sacrificing herself to ensure Tris can escape.

Tris flees Dauntless soldiers, among whom are her friends. At length, she reaches her family and the abusive Marcus. After being patched up, Tris moves to save them. She realizes that interrupting the transmitters is the way to do so, which will require infiltrating Dauntless headquarters.

Chapter 37 & 38

The group makes for Dauntless headquarters. Along the way, the company realizes what Tris has endured to become the young woman who can lead them. She contemplates the nature of bravery along the way before leading the group, under fire, to the computers. Her father sacrifices himself to ensure the mission's success, and Tris encounters Four.

Tris and Four fight. She gets the worse end of the encounter until she manages to break him through the programmed conditioning.

Chapter 39

Four emerges from the haze and kisses Tris before interrupting the transmitters. The emotional impacts of the night begin to tell on those still alive, as do the personal impacts of thwarting a violent coup and the upheaval concomitant with the failure of the coup.

ANALYSIS OF A KEY CHARACTER

Tris

The protagonist, Beatrice "Tris" Prior, is a fairly common coming-of-age heroine. Relatively nondescript of appearance, she facilitates easy readerly identification with her; similarly easing of identification is the sense of her as a uniquely special person. She is Divergent, unbound by the prescribed norms and thought-restricting principles of her society, and powerfully so; it is that difference that allows her to act and to save others. In it, she fulfills wishes for the likely young-adult readers, who will often view themselves as chafing at restriction and possessed of something special that allows them to transcend socially imposed boundaries.

Of note is the emblematic nature of the character name. "Beatrice," going back to Shakespeare and Dante, indicates blessedness, marking it as an appropriate name for the protagonist. It is expected that the focal character will be somehow special. Too, the surname Prior carries a double meaning; it indicates both "before" and a position of religious authority. Beatrice is blessed before the beginning of the novel, and her Abnegation upbringing and leading people out of the wilderness or ruined and war-torn future Chicago carry substantially religious overtones. The names of other characters in the series may serve similar functions that are worth untangling.

CONCLUSION

It is true that there are some problems with Divergent. Some of the action in the later chapters feels rushed, and the obviousness of setup for sequels in the final passages is somewhat grating. The adherence of a number of the characters to the standard tropes of the young-adult, coming-of-age genre is perhaps too rigid. Even so, there are a number of themes in the book that will be of interest to those who teach the expected young-adult readers of the novel, and the core messages of the text are of the sort that bear repeating. As such, Veronica Roth's debut novel, Divergent, comes off as a worthwhile piece of writing that many people will do well to read. If Roth continues to write so well, she will earn a place among the canon of young-adult writers not only of her own time, but for all time. It is something to which to look forward.

CPSIA information can be obtained at www.ICGtesting.com
Printed in the USA
BVOW08s1255200415

396876BV00024B/329/P

9 781500 929190